# The Skeleton
## That Would Not Rest

by Anne Schraff

**Perfection Learning® Corporation**
Logan, Iowa 51546

Cover Design: Mark Hagenberg

Cover Image Credit: Getty Images®

For information, contact:
**Perfection Learning® Corporation**
1000 North Second Avenue, P.O. Box 500,
Logan, Iowa 51546-0500.
Phone: 1-800-831-4190 • Fax: 1-800-543-2745
perfectionlearning.com

Paperback ISBN 0-7891-6576-7
Reinforced Library Binding ISBN 0-7569-4610-7

1 2 3 4 5 6 PP 09 08 07 06 05

1    "HERE'S WHERE THE KOI POND is going to be," 16-year-old Luke Payson said as he drove his shovel into the ground.

"What do we need koi for?" 14-year-old Rhea asked her brother. "And, oh, what are koi anyway?"

"Fish—like carp. Mom thinks it'd be nice to have a koi pond. She said it would be relaxing to watch the fish," Luke said.

"Why not just get a fish tank?" Rhea asked.

"Got me," Luke replied. "Sure would be a lot easier to get a tank than to dig all day. But this is what Mom wants."

As Luke's steel shovel went into the ground, there was a screeching sound as the metal hit something hard.

"Ewwww!" Rhea cried. "What was *that*? It almost sounded like a scream! Maybe there's a gopher down there and you hit him in the head!"

"I don't think so," Luke said. "The earth

is too hard around here for a gopher. They like softer, greener pastures. I did hit something hard, though. Maybe it's a rock."

Luke started to dig around the object, trying to uncover it. His sister knelt on the ground near the hole and started digging with a small trowel to help the process along.

"Maybe it's a treasure box," Rhea said hopefully. "I mean, wouldn't that be fantastic? Then we'd be rich."

"Yeah, right," Luke said. "Like that's going to happen."

Luke uncovered enough of the object to see it was something round and white. A shiver ran up Luke's spine, a sense of horror. He quickly told himself it wasn't what he was thinking. It wasn't a skull. It couldn't be a skull. It had to be just a white rock or something . . .

Rhea sank back on her heels. Her eyes widened. "Luke . . . *what is that*? It looks almost like . . ."

"No," Luke said firmly, brushing dirt off the object. He said nothing, but he was getting weak in the knees. There was no mistaking what he had uncovered now. He could see the empty eye sockets of the skull.

"Luke!" Rhea screamed, jumping back. She was on her feet in a second, running toward the house. "Mommmm!" she shouted. "Mommmmm!"

Luke remained there, staring in disbelief into the hole. He couldn't believe what he was looking at. The Paysons had just bought the house and had been living there for only a week. The previous owners—the Asburys—were a nice elderly couple that had lived in the house for 40 years. Surely they would have known if somebody had buried a body in their backyard!

Rhea came back, trailing their mother, who walked ahead. Rhea did not want to get too close to the skull again.

"Luke, what is going on? Rhea said something about a skull . . ." their mother began. Rhea had the reputation for embellishing stories quite often, so Mrs. Payson had a healthy disrespect for her tales.

"She's right, Mom," Luke said, trying to keep his voice calm. "I was digging for the koi pond when my shovel hit a skull."

"The skull screamed when Luke hit it, Mom," Rhea said excitedly. "I heard it! It was bloodcurdling!"

"Oh, honestly," their mother scoffed. She drew closer to the hole and peered in for herself. "Are you sure it's not one of those plastic skulls they sell in the Halloween stores? Those can be very lifelike, you know . . ."

"I think it's a real one, Mom," Luke said. "I don't want to mess with it any further. There could be . . . you know . . . a whole skeleton down there. I don't think I should dig anymore."

Rhea clamped her hands over her mouth at the horror of it. She turned around and raced back into the house to call everyone she knew to share the terrible news.

"We'd better call the police," Luke said to his mom.

"Yes, of course," his mother said. "Oh, how dreadful. I love this house, and now something like this happens! How could it be? The Asburys lived here *forever*! How could there be a dead body in their yard?"

The police and a coroner arrived at the house on Peppercorn Lane. They strung yellow police tape around the area and labeled it a crime scene.

"So, how long have you people lived here?" Sergeant Jim Arthur, one of the police officers, asked.

"We just moved here from San Diego. We have only been living here for a week," Luke and Rhea's mother replied. "But we bought the house a month ago."

"We bought the house from the Asbury family," their father continued. "The Asburys raised all their kids here. We're really shocked about all this."

"Ah, yes. Jim and Madge Asbury. They lived here for years and years. I knew them well. Jim was my troop leader in the Boy Scouts," Sergeant Arthur said. "So now, was the area where your son was digging covered by anything when you moved in? Like paving stones or landscaping?"

"A rose garden," Mrs. Payson said.

"We had to clear the bushes out before I started digging," Luke said.

"Did the soil look stable? Like there

were no recent disturbances?" Sergeant Arthur asked.

"Yeah. The rose bushes looked like they had been there for a while," Luke said.

"How could something like this have happened, Sergeant?" his mother asked. "Has there been a murder in this town or a missing person's case?"

Sergeant Arthur shrugged. "Not that I know of. But the investigation has just started. We'll see where it leads us," he said.

The police continued digging for the rest of the day. They uncovered an entire skeleton, but they did not remove the remains right away. They took photographs and carefully searched for clues in the surrounding dirt.

Luke and Rhea's mother called Madge Asbury with the news. "You will never guess what has just happened, Mrs. Asbury! My son, Luke, was digging out in the backyard, and he uncovered a skeleton! Right where the rose garden used to be!"

"Oh, my goodness!" Mrs. Asbury gasped. "How in the world did a dead body end up in the backyard? We've been there for 40 years, every day, except for our vacations. And we'd only be gone for a week or so on vacation. Who on earth would bury a dead person in our yard? I suppose the police will want to question us."

"I imagine so," Luke and Rhea's mother replied. "Sergeant Jim Arthur is helping out with the investigation."

"Well, I will contact him immediately. Thanks for letting us know, Mrs. Payson."

Darkness settled, and the coroner took the remains away. The police continued working. They searched the entire area throughout the night and even into the next day.

Sunday evening, after the police had finally left, Luke and Rhea's father tried to steer the dinner conversation away from the grisly find in the backyard. But Rhea did not want to talk about anything else.

"I wish we could move," Rhea wailed. "It's going to be so horrible living here knowing that a dead body was in our yard—that some murderer came here and buried it!"

"Don't be silly, Rhea," her dad scolded. "Naturally, we're all upset by what's happened. But once this is all over, this will be a perfectly wonderful place to live! Just like we believed it would be when we bought the house."

Rhea ignored the spaghetti and meatballs on her plate even though the meal was one of her favorites. "It's probably haunted! The whole house is probably haunted! I just hate the thought of going to bed and having nightmares about it!" she said.

"The police took the remains away, Rhea," her mother pointed out. "We have to do our best to just forget about it."

"I don't think I'll ever forget the sound the shovel made when it hit the skull," Luke said, shuddering. He knew the moment he spoke that it had been a mistake, given Rhea's emotional state. Both of Luke's parents rolled their eyes at his remark.

"I heard it too," Rhea said. "It was like a scream. The skull screamed! I bet we heard the spirit of the dead person!"

"Rhea, please!" her mother said sharply. "This is an unfortunate event, but your father is right. Once this entire ordeal is over, our home will be a nice place to live. Besides, moving anytime soon is out of the question. Your father and I have put all of our money into this house."

"Yeah," their father said, trying to be cheerful. "Remember how much you liked your bedroom with the large windows?"

"Well, I don't like it anymore," Rhea said. "My window looks right into the backyard where the body was!"

..............................................

Later that evening, Rhea could still not get the skull out of her mind. "Luke, we destroyed the final resting place of that skeleton. Don't you see? Our backyard is like a burial ground. We messed with—whoever was buried there—and now some angry spirit is probably wandering around . . ."

"Aw, come on, Rhea. We didn't mean to do anything bad. There's not some avenging ghost after us. The dead guy we found might not have even been murdered. I'll bet there were a couple of drifters going down the railroad track, and one of them died or something. The other guy didn't know what to do, so he just found a place and buried his friend. The Asburys were probably away on vacation during the burial, which would explain why they didn't know about it," Luke said.

Rhea listened but didn't say anything. Then, she grimly walked upstairs to her bedroom.

She didn't appear to believe the story. Luke wasn't even sure if he believed it himself. It sounded plausible, but it was only a guess. He had hoped it might calm Rhea down. Once she got a notion in her head, she was like a dog with a bone. She wouldn't let go and made life miserable for everybody around her.

Luke slowly walked upstairs to his bedroom. He wasn't looking forward to resuming work on the koi pond. Luke wasn't too excited about digging anywhere in the yard now.

Maybe that skull wasn't the only human remains on the property. Maybe something terrible had happened here and more than one person had died.

Maybe, Luke thought, the Asburys weren't the nice couple they seemed to be.

Late Sunday night, long after the Paysons had gone to bed, a strange, mournful sound came from the backyard. Luke climbed from his bed and walked fearfully to the window. His mom soon appeared in his doorway, her robe clutched tight around her.

"*Luke, do you hear that?*" she asked in a quavering voice.

"Yeah," Luke said. "Somebody's crying out there . . ." Luke grabbed a coat off the back of a chair and slipped it on.

"No," his mother cried, "don't go out there!"

2 LUKE HADN'T SEEN anything from the window, but he wanted to investigate the sound. "Mom, I'm just going to take a look around. There's a lot of moonlight, so I'll be able to see the whole backyard . . ."

"Luke!" his mother said suddenly, "maybe the crying isn't coming from the backyard. Maybe that's Rhea crying in her room. She's probably having nightmares. Poor little thing. This has upset her so much!"

Luke and his mother went down the hall to Rhea's room. The door was open, and Rhea was standing at her window staring into the backyard. She turned at the sound of Luke and her mother's footsteps in the hall. "Did you hear it too?" she asked in a shrill, shaky voice.

"Yes. We thought it was you. Have you been crying, darling?" her mother asked, going into the room and reaching for her daughter with a comforting hand.

Rhea evaded her mother's attempts to console her. "I wasn't crying! It was somebody, or some*thing*, down there. Our yard is haunted! We've disturbed the grave and now . . . now . . . ."

Luke's father, who was awakened by the noise, joined them. He was in his pajamas, barefoot. "What in the world is going on? Why is everybody standing around at this hour?" he asked.

"Didn't you hear that crying, Rob?" Luke and Rhea's mother asked. "It woke us all up. It sounded like it might be coming from the backyard."

Luke and Rhea's father was the soundest sleeper in the family. Their mother had said several times that if an earthquake knocked the house off of its foundation, he would sleep through it all. "I didn't hear anything," he said.

"Oh, I hate this place so much," Rhea groaned.

Luke's dad looked at Luke. "I'll get a sweater on. Luke and I will go out there and see what's making the ruckus," he said.

"No," Luke and Rhea's mother objected, "I don't want anybody going outside."

"Come on, Ellie," their dad objected, slipping on shoes and then leading the way downstairs. "We're all acting like a bunch of scared little rabbits. You guys probably just heard a dove cooing outside or maybe an owl shrieking. Those things can make a lot of noise."

Their father headed down the stairs while the other three trailed closely behind. "Cooing from a dove in the middle of the night?" Rhea demanded. "Honestly, Dad."

"Rhea, you and your mother stay here. You can watch from the kitchen window," their father ordered. "Luke, come on."

The two men stepped outside. They glanced around the moonlit backyard. The police had tried to cover all the holes they had made, but the yard was still a mess. "Luke," his dad said, "first chance we get, we've got to plant around here. Make this place look like a home instead of a construction site. We need to get that koi pond in too. The sooner we do that stuff, the sooner your mother and sister will get over this."

"Sure, Dad," Luke replied.

Luke couldn't hear the sobbing sound anymore. He walked alongside his father, cocking his ear to the soft wind. He would have suspected the crying he had heard was only his imagination, but his mom and Rhea had heard it too.

It had to have been something outside.

They drew near the place where the skeleton had been found. The hole had been filled in, but Luke still recognized the spot. It was burned into his mind. It was just a few steps from the old oak tree's knot.

"Luke, does the ground seem damp to you?" his dad asked in a startled voice.

Luke glanced up at the cloudless sky. "It didn't rain, though," he said.

"But it's wet right here, like someone watered the soil. Luke, this is where the body was buried, isn't it?" his dad said. He knelt down and stirred the damp soil with his fingertip. "Man, there are tiny little black seeds buried here, in a line. Like somebody was trying to plant something, you know, where the . . . grave was . . ."

Luke got a nervous chill even though it wasn't cold. He imagined some ghost trying to restore the dignity of the grave by planting flowers or something. It didn't make any sense, but . . .

"Luke, don't mention this—the damp ground and seeds—to your mother or Rhea," Mr. Payson cautioned. "They're spooked enough . . ."

They walked back toward the house in silence. Luke couldn't shake the image from his mind, some ghost spraying seeds over the ravaged gravesite, trying to heal the brutal disruption that had occurred. He struggled to push the disturbing image from his mind. "Dad, do you think the police will tell us the name of the dead person? I mean, once they make an identification?" Luke asked.

"Yeah. Jim Arthur promised to keep us posted," his dad answered. "But he said it might not be easy to identify the remains. I guess they go through a list of missing people and try to match the dental records to the body."

The two walked up the back stairs and met Rhea and her mother, who were waiting at the back door.

"Everything is cool," Luke's dad said cheerfully. "Let's all go back to bed and try to get some sleep. Must have been a bird or some animal. We're so used to living in the city that we're not used to country sounds."

"Yeah," Luke said. Their mom seemed relieved, but Rhea seemed unconsoled.

......................................................

The next morning Luke and Rhea waited for the bus that took them about seven miles to Blue Mountain Regional High School. Rhea was a freshman and Luke was a junior. The school served the kids from the surrounding small towns including Hardy and adjoining Appleton.

Rhea was very social, and in one week she had already made several friends. Luke, after the first week, still had no friends. It was harder for him to connect with people. He felt like an outsider.

When Luke walked into his history class on Monday morning, a husky suntanned boy approached him. "Hey, they found a dead body at your place, didn't they? You're Luke Payson, right? I saw your name in the paper. They said you dug up the body."

Luke groaned to himself. The local

newspaper had little to talk about except the local 4-H activities, so the discovery of a skeleton was big news. Hardy had a population of only 700, and nobody had been murdered in the town for 80 years. The student thrust a paper at Luke. The headline read, "Teenager finds skeleton in family backyard." Then the boy identified himself. "I'm Casey Pike."

A pretty dark-haired girl tugged at Luke's elbow. "*Wow*, you found the body?" she asked.

"Yeah," Luke said. He wished he hadn't found anything.

"I'm Nickell Polito," the girl said. "I bet you jumped when you saw the skeleton! That's so horrible."

Well, Luke thought to himself, at least kids are talking to me now. The dead body got me introduced around my junior class!

"It *was* weird," Luke confessed.

"I wonder who it is," Casey said. "Nobody is missing around Hardy except the teacher's kid." Casey grinned a little at the humor he suddenly found in the macabre situation. "Hey, you're in trouble if you find our history teacher's kid in your backyard!"

Another boy, who Luke learned was named Rocky, laughed too.

"Hey," Rocky said, "didn't an old couple used to live there? The Asburys, I think? Now *there's* a family. They had three kids, but all of them moved away. That's what the parents said, anyway. Maybe they never did move away. Maybe they all got murdered and buried in the backyard. Hey, Luke, maybe you'll find other skeletons out there!" Casey roared at that scenario.

"Rocky, don't be stupid," Nickell said. "The Asburys are nice people. Their kids all moved to Los Angeles."

"So they said," Casey interjected. "I guess that might be true. Any kid living in this creepy town wants to get out of here as quick as they can. This place closes in on you like a steel trap. I'm getting out as soon as I graduate."

"Not me," Nickell said. "I love it here. I love going biking and hiking in the mountains. I love seeing deer come almost to our back door to drink out of the river. I go to the city occasionally to visit my grandparents, and I hate it. The stinky traffic, the noise, everybody rushing around and being rude."

Luke instantly liked Nickell. He smiled at her. "We used to live in San Diego. It's a great place, but it got so crowded where we were. Dad worked eight miles from our condo, and it sometimes took him two hours to get home in rush hour traffic. My high school was so jammed with students that we couldn't even get to the lockers," he said.

Casey did not want to drop the subject of the skeleton. "What did the dead body look like, Luke?"

"Like a skull. White," Luke said.

"Did you scream?" Casey asked, still grinning.

"No, but I was kinda shocked," Luke said.

"I bet it's weird living there now, huh? I mean, your yard is sort of like a cemetery," he said gleefully.

"Don't be silly, Casey," Nickell said. "Luke is going to think we're all fools around here if you don't stop talking like that."

The history teacher—Ms. Fischer—walked into the classroom, and Luke's newfound friends dispersed. She was a tall, reed-thin woman who looked drawn and weary. Luke had heard that she had been teaching at Blue Mountain High for 15 years.

Ms. Fischer talked about the colonial period in American history. She told a lot of colorful details about life at that time for ordinary people. Luke liked her. She made history interesting.

As the class came to a close, Ms. Fischer seemed to be staring at Luke. It made him uncomfortable. Luke remembered what Casey had said about the teacher's missing child.

After the bell dismissing class rang, Ms. Fischer approached Luke. "I need a word with you, Luke," she said.

When everybody else had left the room, the teacher asked in a tense voice, "You saw the skull?"

"Yes," Luke said.

Ms. Fischer seemed almost distraught. She reached out and grasped Luke's shoulder. "Please tell me . . . could it have been the skull of a 16-year-old boy?" she asked.

**3** "I'M SORRY; I don't know," Luke admitted. "I couldn't, you know, tell from what I saw. We called the police, and they were the ones who uncovered the whole body."

"My son was 16 when he disappeared. It was about a year ago," Ms. Fischer said, baring her soul's anguish in a way a teacher had never done with Luke before. It seemed strange and unsettling. "I haven't heard a word from him since. I assumed he ran away because we'd been having some problems. But surely he would have contacted me. At least a phone call or something."

"Sergeant Jim Arthur is running the investigation. You had better call him, Ms. Fischer," Luke said. "He'd be able to, you know, tell the details about the . . . the body." Luke felt sorry for the woman. Her eyes were dark with tears.

"Yes, I'll do that," she said. "Thank you, Luke."

When Luke got outside the classroom, Casey and Nickell were waiting for him.

"What'd she want, dude?" Casey asked. "You in trouble already?"

Luke didn't want to discuss the teacher's personal misery with anybody. Least of all Casey Pike, whom he already disliked. "She's just worried about her son," he said.

"Ben Fischer was cool," Casey said.

Nickell sniffed. "He was a good kid until he started hanging out with you and Rocky, Casey. Then his grades went downhill, and he got in trouble with his mom."

"Ben didn't have a fun life," Casey said. "Imagine what it was like for the poor guy. Getting hassled by old lady Fischer in school as his teacher, then going home and she's hassling him again as his mom. No wonder the guy lost it. That's enough to make anybody take off."

"You riding home on the bus, Luke?" Nickell asked.

"Yeah. My sister and I both are," Luke said.

"I've got a car," Casey said. "I'm dropping

Nickell off. Why don't you and your sister come along?"

"You've got your own car?" Luke asked in amazement. Luke didn't count on having his own car until he had made enough money to buy one. And that probably wouldn't happen until after high school.

"Yeah," Casey said with a grin. "My old man made a deal with me. As long as I don't slip below a C, I can keep the car. Come on, I'll show you the sights on the way home. Show you what we do for fun around here."

Luke found Rhea and they both met Casey and Nickell in the school parking lot.

The four climbed into the car, and Casey sped onto the main highway. Luke was already sorry that he had accepted the ride.

To make matters worse, Casey did not take the route home that the bus took.

"Hey, where are we going?" Luke asked.

"We're taking the scenic route," Casey said.

Nickell looked concerned. "Casey, you're not going down past the homeless camp again, are you? You promised you wouldn't! I'm warning you, Casey Pike, if you pull something like you did before . . ." she sounded angry.

Casey laughed as he swung off the main road and down a dirt road leading through a meadow.

"We're gonna shake up the weirdos," Casey said.

"Casey," Nickell cried, "you promised you'd never do that again!"

"Hey, I just want to show Luke and his little sister what we do to keep Hardy clean," Casey said, ignoring Nickell's pleas.

"What are you doing?" Luke demanded. "I've got my 14-year-old sister here. I don't want anything weird going on."

"Ahhh, keep your shirt on, dude," Casey said. "See, there's a makeshift camp where the bums hang out. Everybody in Hardy is sick and tired of the dirty, lazy creeps. My dad says they're a big nuisance. He'd like to see them all run out of town. They make the place look trashy. Why should a bunch of lazy slobs ruin our town? They just need a little shaking up so they don't get too comfortable around here."

Casey turned sharply and a small camp on the river came into view. There were three or four people standing around.

"Casey! Don't!" Nickell screamed.

Casey gunned the engine and went roaring toward the four people as if he intended to run them over. The four scattered, running for their lives.

"Man, what are you doing?" Luke yelled. "You're going to kill somebody!"

Casey swerved just in time, roaring with laughter, throwing a spray of dirt and pebbles after the fleeing people. "I just put a scare in them. Now they won't feel so safe around here. Got to make them nervous. Then maybe they'll move to another place. Don't you get it? They're like roaches. Scare them off so they infest somebody else's house," he said.

Rhea gave Luke a dark look that said, next time, keep your rotten friends to yourself! Luke shrugged apologetically. He hadn't liked Casey the first few minutes after he met him, but Luke never suspected he would do something like this. This was sick and evil.

"You are totally disgusting, Casey. I'll never ride with you again!" Nickell yelled.

Casey chuckled. "That's what she says now, but the girl loves me. She can't help herself," he said.

Casey dropped off Nickell first, and then he let off Luke and Rhea. Luke made a silent promise that he'd never make this mistake again. From now on, until he had a car of his own, it would be the bus.

As Luke and his sister walked toward their house, Rhea glanced around all the open land on the property. "If somebody wanted to bury a body, why did they pick a spot so close to the house?" she asked.

"I don't know," Luke said.

"I hope we don't hear any more weird noises like the ones we heard last night," Rhea said. "Maybe it was just some kind of an animal, but it sure sounded like a human being crying. It just sent chills up my back . . ."

"I don't think we'll be bothered anymore," Luke said, just to reassure his sister.

A smile flickered on Rhea's face. "You know what? I met the coolest guy in my science class today. That class has freshmen and sophomores, and Carlos is a sophomore. He's not a jerk like most of the boys in my class. He started talking to me right away."

Luke smiled. He was glad Rhea had found a distraction. He had found a special friend too—Nickell Polito. He really liked her, and he felt pretty sure that she liked him.

"Sergeant Arthur called today," Luke and Rhea's mother said when they walked into the house. "He wanted to let us know that there was still no identification of that body."

"Ms. Fischer, my history teacher, told me her son has been missing for a year. She's really worried that the remains might . . . you know . . . be him," Luke said.

"Oh, my goodness," his mother replied. "I can't imagine anything worse than having a child missing and having to wonder every time there's a body found . . ."

"I told her to call Sergeant Arthur," Luke continued. "I guess they're checking out everybody who went missing in the last couple of years."

"You know, Luke," his mother said thoughtfully, "I was thinking. I don't want the koi pond where we planned it. I'd like to just plant a bush there or something. You can start a hole for the koi pond on the other side of the house. I think that'd be best, don't you?"

"Yeah, Mom," Luke said. But for a terrible moment he thought about Rocky's ugly prediction. *Maybe you'll find more skeletons out there!*

After several days of waiting, the police informed the Paysons that the skeletal remains were from a male who had died within the last 12 months. But the dead body did not belong to any missing person from the area.

So the skeleton did not belong to Ms. Fischer's son, Ben. Luke was relieved to hear that. That meant that there was still hope that Ben was alive.

Unfortunately, the skeleton was *somebody's* son.

The Paysons calmed down somewhat as the days passed, and it seemed that life might return to normal. But then, on Friday night, Luke was awakened by something. He wasn't sure what he had heard that woke him up, but it seemed to come from the backyard. He got out of bed and went to the window, expecting to see a pair of raccoons rummaging through the garbage pail.

Although a storm was threatening, the moon was still in a clear place. It shed bright light over the valley. Luke stared into the backyard for a few minutes. Then he caught his breath in a gasp.

Next to the large oak tree stood a shadowy figure. A person was standing quite close to where the skeleton had been buried. Luke wasn't sure if the figure was a man or a woman. But it was a person for sure, lurking around the burial place.

Luke went into the hall and turned on the backyard light. The powerful beam lit up the whole area. He rushed back to the window, but he didn't see the figure anymore. The light had apparently scared the person away.

Luke pulled on jeans and shoes and went outside.

It was cool and windy, and the

branches of the trees were rustling. The moon disappeared behind some black clouds, and only its bright edge still showed.

"Who's there?" Luke shouted. He didn't expect an answer, but suddenly a figure darted from behind the oak tree and ran into the woods.

"Hey!" Luke shouted, taking off after the figure. He ran into the woods too. After about 30 yards he stopped and looked around. The underbrush, a tangle of vines, made it difficult to walk.

Just as Luke turned to the sound of a twig breaking underfoot, somebody right behind him gave him a violent shove. It sent him sprawling into a berry patch. Luke caught his breath and scrambled to his feet. He turned around in circles searching desperately for the attacker. But it was to no avail. The person had vanished into the deep, dark woods.

Luke looked down at his hands. They were bleeding.

4 WHEN LUKE FELL, he gashed his hand against a rock. Blood ran from his palm. His other hand was scratched by a thorn from the berry patch. Neither wound was serious, but Luke was shaken by the incident. Now there was no doubt that someone was out there. Could it be someone who had information about the dead body?

Luke's immediate reaction, as he walked back to the house, was to alert his family and call the police. But then he had second thoughts. Maybe the intruder was just somebody from the homeless camp looking for scraps. It could have been. Those people had enough trouble from guys like Casey Pike harassing them. If Luke reported that he'd been attacked, the police would probably swoop down on the homeless camp.

Plus, Luke did not really have a good description of his attacker. He could have sworn he saw long hair on the dark figure in the yard, but he wasn't sure. Maybe it was some poor, frightened, homeless girl who was just hungry.

Luke decided not to mention the incident to anyone.

......................................................

On Saturday morning, Luke started another hole for his mom's koi pond. Rhea nervously helped him. Luke could tell that with every shovelful of dirt, Rhea expected they would uncover something horrible.

"What if there are more bodies? What if this used to be a cemetery or something? Have you ever thought of that—that this was some old boot hill?" Rhea cried, sharing her darkest fears.

"No," Luke said. "That couldn't be. The remains we found were less than a year old. The Asburys lived here for 40 years, and they were digging all the time to plant trees and shrubs. They never uncovered anything."

"Luke, you didn't hear anything weird last night, did you?" Rhea asked, suddenly changing the subject.

"Weird?" Luke repeated. "Like what?"

"I don't know. Something woke me up around midnight," Rhea said. "I know you're going to laugh, but when I looked out the window I was almost sure I saw a person in the yard . . ."

"Why didn't you say something before now?" Luke asked.

"I felt foolish. Plus, I wasn't sure. It could have been my imagination, but I thought I saw somebody creeping around the yard. It was somebody in dark clothes and, I don't know, maybe it was a woman," Rhea said. "Maybe she was the one crying a few nights ago."

"Yeah," Luke said, "I saw somebody too, Rhea. I went outside and a little way into the woods, and this person, whoever it was, was running to get away. He or she knocked me down . . ."

Rhea's eyes grew wide. "Oh, Luke! Don't you see what's happening? The murderer is stalking us! He or she knows we found the dead body and is now coming after us!" she cried.

"No, Rhea, I don't think so. I think it was just a drifter from the homeless camp looking for food. I think it was a woman or a girl. Remember when Casey Pike hassled those people? If we report that a homeless person was in our backyard, then people like Casey will have even more reason to make the lives of homeless people miserable," Luke said.

Rhea nodded, calming down. "Yeah, I bet you're right. That camp isn't far from here, is it? I felt so sorry for them. I told Carlos what had happened, and he said sometimes Casey and his friends take their hunting rifles out to the homeless camp and shoot over the heads of the people. Just to terrorize them. The homeless people never report it to the police, though, because they're scared of the law," she said.

"That's really ugly," Luke said bitterly. "Casey Pike is a disgusting creep."

"Yeah," Rhea said. "Imagine having to live in a cardboard box and eat scraps. That kind of life is bad enough without creeps hassling you too."

On Monday, Luke ran into Nickell

before history. "Hey, Nickell."

"Hey, Luke. Did you have a good weekend?" she asked.

"Yeah, it was okay. Didn't do much. Hey, you wouldn't happen to like biking, would you?" Luke asked nervously.

"Oh, yeah, I love it," Nickell said. "I've got a mountain bike I use all the time around here."

"I was thinking maybe we could go biking on Saturday morning," Luke said. "Maybe you could show me some of the sights. My mom could pack us a lunch. She makes great lunches."

"That sounds good," Nickell said enthusiastically. "You can't believe how many really nice little nooks and crannies we've got around here. The oldest house in Hardy is hidden in a little wooded area; it looks like the gingerbread house in *Hansel and Gretel*."

"Awesome! I'll be over at your place around 10:00," Luke said.

Casey Pike came walking along as they were finishing their conversation. "What's happening with you guys?" he asked.

"Luke and I are going biking on Saturday. I'm going to show him all the sights around here," Nickell said.

"That should take about three minutes," Casey smirked.

"Come on, Casey," Nickell snapped. "We've got some of the most beautiful scenery in the state, and you know it."

"Borrrrring," Casey said.

Nickell rolled her eyes and then caught up to a girlfriend, leaving Luke alone with Casey.

In front of Nickell, Casey seemed very cool and good-natured. But now his smile vanished as if it were a mask suddenly ripped from his face. "What's going on here? What do you think you're doing?"

"Come again?" Luke asked.

"You're moving in on my girlfriend, dude. That's not how we do things. Maybe where you're from, guys steal girlfriends, but around here, we don't rip off another guy's chick," Casey said hotly.

"Nickell's not your girlfriend," Luke said.

"You're a slippery snake, aren't you, dude?" Casey said bitterly. "I was just getting close to her, so close that she'd be eating out of my hand pretty soon. Don't ruin this for me."

"History class is going to start in a

minute," Luke said. "I'm going in."

Luke took his seat in class, calm on the outside, but shaken on the inside. He saw a lot of hatred in Casey's face. The guy looked like he was capable of anything . . .

After classes ended for the day, as Luke and Rhea waited for the bus, Casey and two of his friends came walking up. "Hey, Luke," Casey said, showing his affable side again because he was with other people. "My buddies here think maybe you robbed some cemetery and buried the stiff on your property just to get attention."

Luke ignored the question. Seeing they couldn't get a rise out of Luke, they started picking on Rhea.

"Did you see the skeleton, Rhea? Were all the parts there?" Casey asked.

"Did you see any blood?" Rocky asked her.

"Go away," Rhea snapped.

"You can really get in trouble messing with skeletons," Casey said. "The spirits of the dead come after you."

"Look, you guys, just get lost," Luke finally said.

"What would you do if the angry ghost came in your room late at night, Rhea?" Casey asked.

"I told you guys to get lost," Luke said, getting angry.

"Where's the stupid bus?" Rhea asked impatiently.

When the bus finally appeared, the three boys roared with mocking laughter.

"I hate this place so much," Rhea said as she sat down.

"Just blow it off," Luke said. "It'll all get stale for Casey and his friends pretty soon."

"It's not just that," Rhea said. "Kids in my classes are always asking me gross questions about the skeleton. Carlos is really nice about it, but some of the kids can be annoying."

"I know it's tough, but you can survive it," Luke said.

"I don't see why we can't just move!" Rhea said.

"Rhea, get real," Luke said softly, so the other kids on the bus wouldn't hear the conversation. "Dad has his office all set up, and this is a great place to live."

The bus dropped off Luke and Rhea, and they walked up the driveway. The old two-story house they lived in had been shabby when they bought it, but after a new roof and fresh paint, it looked beautiful. The small, dark kitchen had been remodeled into a modern stainless-steel delight for their mom. Everything was exactly as they wanted it.

Except for the skeleton in the rose garden.

Luke went into the house first. "Hi, Mom, we're home!" he shouted. This was their father's day to make his hour-long commute into his office, so he wouldn't return until late. Their mom spent her days writing a historical novel. She was doing research on the Internet, finding facts about 18th-century France among the wealthy class.

"Mom, where are you?" Rhea shouted after she walked in. Usually their mother was right there to greet them and ask about their day.

"She's probably outside admiring the new hole I made for the koi pond," Luke said.

Rhea followed Luke outside, but their mother was nowhere in sight.

"Luke, where could she be?" Rhea asked, a hint of worry creeping into her voice. "There's her car in the driveway. So she didn't drive anywhere . . ."

"Mom!" Luke shouted in a louder voice. "Hey, I bet I know! She probably got so tired doing all that research that she took a nap. I bet she's up there sleeping!"

Luke and his sister hurried up the winding staircase to their parents' bedroom.

"Mom!" Rhea shouted.

"Rhea, don't get so excited. You want to scare her?" Luke cautioned.

But their mother wasn't in the bedroom. The bed was completely made. The room was empty and silent.

"Well, maybe she took a walk," Luke said. "You know how she loves to walk around, observing nature and stuff. She probably just went into the woods a little ways and got hung up watching birds or something." Luke forced a cheerful smile, but inside he felt scared. His mom, walking by herself in those woods? Under the thick canopy of trees? Where the dark figure had attacked Luke?

"Mom!" Rhea was screaming as they went into the woods. "Mom, where are you?"

5 BOTH LUKE and Rhea continued shouting as they advanced into the woods. And then, from a short distance away, they heard her voice. "Over here, darlings."

"She sounds okay," Luke said, weak with relief.

Their mother suddenly appeared, a smile on her face. "What's all the yelling about?" she asked.

"Mom!" Rhea cried. "You had us worried sick! We got home, and you weren't there! You weren't anywhere! We looked all over for you, and we were so scared! What are you doing by yourself in this horrible, spooky place?"

"Oh, sweetheart, I'm sorry," their mother said, giving Rhea a hug. "But these woods aren't spooky. They're magical. I've never seen so many birds! Bobwhites and scarlet tanagers. I was writing, and I just needed a break to stretch my legs. I kept walking farther and farther, and the time got away from me." Her smile deepened. "And then I met this lovely girl."

"What girl?" Luke asked.

"Oh, I've never seen her before. Quite thin, but lovely. She seemed about your age, Luke. She probably goes to your high school. She said her name was Rain. I must say I've never met a girl named Rain before, but it seems like people are always coming up with unusual names these days. She was delightful," their mother said.

Luke and Rhea exchanged a puzzled look.

"Actually, she said she was a neighbor of ours," their mother continued. "She said she knew the Asburys very well. She helped them plant that rose garden. The one, you know, we tore up for the koi pond. She seemed a bit sad that the roses weren't there anymore . . ."

"Did she know what we found there?" Luke asked. "I mean, had she heard about . . ."

"Oh, we didn't talk about that," their mother said. "I didn't want to ruin a pleasant conversation. Anyway, I promised her we'd consider putting in new roses. She seemed happy about that."

The three of them walked back toward the house. Mrs. Payson continued her happy chatter. "I've never met a young girl before who seemed so mature. I wonder if she's in any of your classes, Luke."

"I don't know. I haven't met anybody named Rain yet," Luke said.

"She has these incredible green eyes and very pale, creamy skin. Just lovely skin. You know, as I was looking at her, I got an excellent description of Yvette, the heroine in my novel," their mother bubbled.

"You shouldn't go walking in the woods by yourself, Mom," Rhea said grimly.

"Oh, darling, it was broad daylight," their mother said.

"Rhea is right, though, Mom," Luke said. "The other night Rhea and I both saw some figure walking around our backyard. Then it disappeared into the woods."

"You didn't say anything about that," their mother said, looking upset. "If there was a prowler, we should have called the police."

"Well, we figured it was somebody from that homeless camp," Luke said. "I thought it was just some poor, hungry person looking for scraps. I didn't want the police to go after them."

"Oh, that must be the homeless camp Cindy Pike was talking about. I saw her at the grocery store today. Her son Casey is in school with you, Luke. You've probably met him. Cindy said he's popular and friendly. Anyway, Cindy said she and her husband are trying to get the homeless people out of town," their mother said.

"Casey is a creepy guy," Luke said.

"Oh. Well, anyway, Cindy said there's going to be a community meeting to discuss ways of getting rid of the homeless camp. She wants me to go, but I don't think so. The homeless already have enough problems. I feel guilty adding to their troubles," their mother said.

As Luke's mother spoke, Luke found his mind drifting. Who was this girl named Rain? Was she the girl who had shoved him that night in her haste to escape?

....................................................

At dinner that night, Luke said he'd invited Nickell Polito to go biking with him on Saturday morning.

"And *I'm* going to be playing softball. I've been picked for the team already," Rhea said, not wanting to be outdone by her older brother.

"My goodness," their mother said with a pleased grin. "You kids don't waste any time, do you? You've been here less than two weeks! You're already right in the heart of things."

After dinner, Luke joined his father on the swing on the big front porch. The huge, old-fashioned front porch was one thing everybody loved about the house.

"I didn't want to spoil dinner," Luke's father said, "but on the way home today I stopped and had a chat with Sergeant Arthur. He said they've gotten an artist to do a sketch of the young man they found, based on the bones in his face, that sort of thing. They believe he was around 18 and 6 feet tall. Sergeant Arthur wants to get the sketch out on some flyers, you know, to see if anybody recognizes the body."

"Poor guy. I wonder what happened to him," Luke said.

"A bullet in the back of his head," Luke's dad said. "When you first saw the skull, you were looking at the top. He was shot at the base of the skull. Jim Arthur said it's a homicide investigation now. The young fellow was probably murdered."

"So the murderer killed him and then buried him in our backyard? I mean, the Asburys' backyard," Luke said.

"Looks like it. The burial probably happened when the Asburys were on vacation, and when they got home the dirt was settled. Most likely the Asburys never dug there," his dad said.

"But there was a rose garden there," Luke remembered. "Mrs. Asbury said it was planted about a year ago."

"Yes, but you don't have to dig that deep to plant roses, not as deep as you were digging for the koi pond. Anyway, maybe they just missed the skeleton by dumb luck," Luke's dad said.

Luke nodded. "It sure is sad to think

that somebody's son was in our backyard."

"I agree. Some grief-stricken family is probably out there wondering what happened to their boy. That's why Jim Arthur wants to get those flyers all around the country. It might lead to his identity," he said.

"Dad, did you hear about the meeting the Pike family is organizing? They want to try and run the homeless people out of town," Luke asked.

"Yeah. I'm not too keen on that. I drove by the camp, and it's not all that messy. I asked Jim Arthur if there's a crime problem from those people, and he said no. Once in a while they toss pop bottles and stuff, but so do the locals," Mr. Payson said. "This guy, Pike, he's sort of a self-styled leader. I don't believe much of what he's saying."

"His son is a jerk too," Luke said.

"Well, just steer clear of him, Luke. Guys like that are best ignored. Don't give him a reason to get on your case," his Dad suggested.

Luke said nothing, but he was afraid

Casey already had a reason for targeting him. Luke *was* going biking with Nickell. Even though Nickell wasn't Casey's girl, he thought he had rights over her.

........................................................

It had rained on Friday night, but Saturday morning shone bright and clear. Only a misting rain had fallen, so the trails were hard. Luke's mother had packed a picnic lunch of club sandwiches, potato salad, and apple pie. Luke placed it carefully into his backpack where everything comfortably fit in plastic containers.

When Luke pedaled up to the Polito house, he was cordially greeted by Nickell's father. They shook hands as Nickell wheeled her bike from the garage. "You guys have a nice day," Mr. Polito called after Luke and Nickell as they pedaled off.

"There's a turn up ahead," Nickell said. "We'll go right. That takes us to the old historical house. You can hardly see it anymore, though, because it's hidden by brush and trees."

"Who lived in it?" Luke asked.

"Some young couple," Nickell said. "They were the first people who settled around here. The house is made of all these little round stones, and they're different colors—gray, brown, reddish. The couple built their dream house on the river, stone by stone."

Nickell and Luke traveled through a meadow and then, up ahead, Luke saw the tree-lined river where the woods grew much thicker, even thicker than the trees behind the Payson house. "See?" Nickell pointed out. "You can barely see the house."

"I see the stones through the leaves of the trees," Luke said.

They plowed through the vines and brush until they reached the house.

"Look at that," Luke cried. "It *is* like a gingerbread house."

"Yeah, they were both artists, the young couple. They wanted to find an isolated place where they could work, so they came here. See the stained glass window? The girl made it. And he was a stone mason," Nickell said.

"Can we get inside?" Luke asked.

"No, not anymore. The historical

association boarded up the windows, all but that little stained glass one. The doors are nailed shut too. People used to go in and vandalize the place. The historical association is hoping to get some money to restore the house and have tours. They want to make the whole area around here like a park," Nickell said.

"Did they live here for a long time, Nickell?" Luke asked.

"No," Nickell said, her expression turning sad. "They were just in their early twenties when they came here. It took them about two years to build the house. Then, right after they moved in, somebody came and killed the young man. Maybe it was a passing robber. Who knows? Anyway, the murder was never solved. It happened over a hundred years ago."

"What happened to the wife?" Luke asked.

"That's even sadder. She went kind of mad. She lived alone in the house for a while, and then one day she died. They found her body draped over her husband's grave. He was buried right here for a while. But then they moved the man and his wife to the town cemetery. The only thing that remains, besides the house, is this little bronze plaque with their names on them. See it here?"

Luke knelt down and read the plaque carefully, "Steven Wiltgen, 1884–1908, and Rain Wiltgen, 1886–1909, joined in love, joined in eternity."

Luke turned numb.

Rain? *The girl's name was Rain?*

6 "NICKELL, a couple of days ago, my mom was walking behind our house, and she met this girl. And the girl said her name was Rain," Luke said. "I've never heard of anybody named Rain, and now I know two people with that name."

"That *is* weird," Nickell said. "Maybe she saw the plaque and just took the name. Maybe she didn't like her real name. Come on, Luke, I can't wait to show you the waterfall. It's just amazing. Strangers don't even know about it, because it's hidden from the road."

They biked on down the trail until it became too narrow to ride. They walked their bikes about 100 yards until they came to a rocky cliff.

"Wow," Luke said when he saw the sparkling, silvery spray plunging down the face of the white granite. "That's beautiful."

"Yeah," Nickell said. "It's like the falls in

Yosemite National Park, only smaller. It's pretty now, but after a big rain, it's just amazing. The whole cliff side bursts with water."

When they biked away from the falls, they came to a small meadow where they had lunch.

Everything Mrs. Payson had packed was perfect. Luke spread the tablecloth and put out the sandwiches, potato salad, and pie.

"Boy, your mom thought of everything," Nickell said, "even little plastic forks and spoons!"

"And the trash bag that must return with us with every bit of garbage. Mom is an environmental fanatic," Luke said.

They could hear the nearby river becoming a rapids as they ate. Luke was marvelling at the silence, broken only softly by the roar of the river, when another sound overwhelmed everything else. It was a growing roar.

"Motorcycles," Nickell groaned.

"Motorcycles?" Luke echoed in surprise. "How can motorcycles come down that narrow bike trail?"

"They can't. They come in from another direction. Just right over there—see that wide dirt road? Oh, I hate it when those guys come blasting through. It's like they couldn't care less about the natural landscape. They just want to tear everything up," Nickell said.

"Do you know who they are?" Luke asked before the motorcycles appeared.

"Oh, it'll be Casey and Rocky, and probably Johnny Lowden," Nickell said. "It's all my fault. I never should have let Casey know we were coming here today."

The motorcycles roared into view, with Casey Pike in the lead. He ground to a stop near Luke and Nickell and sent bits of mud flying through the air.

"Hey, look at this," Casey said mockingly, "you guys being right here. Small world, eh?"

"Yeah. Small world," echoed Rocky and Johnny as they climbed off their bikes.

"Casey, you are such a pain," Nickell said. "It was nice and peaceful before you showed up."

"Hey, I'm really sorry, Nickell," Casey said without a shred of sincerity.

"You can leave anytime you want, Casey," Nickell said. "We were hoping to see some wildlife, but fat chance of that now!"

"Oh, is Luke here a bird-watcher?" Casey asked mockingly. "Hey, I didn't know that. You like to watch little birdies, dude?"

The other boys joined in the taunting.

"Hey, look quick, Luke. I think I just saw a yellow-bellied sapsucker go by!" Rocky said.

"Hey," Johnny said, "there goes a pea-headed red-headed warbler!"

"Knock it off, you guys," Nickell said. "I'm the bird-watcher. I've always loved birds."

"Hey, did you guys see the little haunted house?" Casey asked. "I'll bet Luke would like to see that, because his house is haunted now too. Right, Luke?"

Luke gave Casey a dirty look.

Casey drew closer. "Hey, Luke, did Nickell tell you how the guy in the little stone house died? Somebody beheaded him. Somebody swung this big axe and lopped his head right off. Maybe it was his wife. She was seen roaming around like a witch even after she died."

"You don't know anything about what happened!" Nickell snapped. "Casey Pike, you're almost 18 years old! When are you going to grow up?"

Casey and the other two finally walked back to their motorcycles and roared off, hurling more mud behind them. Long after they had gone, the stench of the gasoline engines remained.

Nickell sighed, "Good. They're gone."

"There was no truth to what Casey said about the wife, was there?" Luke asked. "I mean, they don't know if she killed her husband, do they?"

"The crime was never solved from what I heard," Nickell said. "There were all kinds of stories. People love to speculate about such things. But they were sweet, artistic people, and I can't imagine her doing such a thing. She was a small, gentle girl from what I've read."

Luke and Nickell finished their lunch and drank the lemonade Nickell had brought. They cleaned up the campsite, and Luke stuffed the trash bag into his backpack for disposal at home.

"You're a lot of fun to be with, Nickell. I had so much fun today that not even those creeps could spoil the day for me."

"Thanks," Nickell said, "I like being with you too. I feel real comfortable around you, and we've only known each other a few days."

Luke had noticed in his high school back home that most of the girls in his classes were always thinking about how they looked. Did their hair look okay? Was their lipstick holding up all right? Nickell wasn't like that. She didn't wear any makeup at all, and her naturally curly hair looked fine all the time.

Nickell seemed like a natural, down-to-earth girl.

"I'm glad we ended up in the same history class," Luke said.

"Me too," Nickell agreed.

As they bicycled along, they heard the distant roar of gunfire. It echoed off the adjoining hills.

"*What was that?*" Luke gasped. "It sounds like an infantry platoon doing maneuvers."

"That's how it sounds around here

during the hunting season. But right now, it's not the hunting season. It must be those jerks who were just hassling us. They're probably taking shots at the road signs. Haven't you noticed how many road signs around here are marked with bullet holes?" Nickell said.

"They're not allowed to do that, are they?" Luke asked. "I mean, that's discharging a firearm illegally, isn't it?"

"Yeah, you're right," Nickell said. "But you've got to understand, Hardy is a small town. Everybody knows everybody else. Like the police chief, Roy Anderson. He's best friends with Casey Pike's dad. They went to school together. In fact, when they were teens, they probably shot at the signs too. The law sort of shrugs this off as harmless kid stuff. You might not understand, though. You've never lived in a small town, Luke. You don't know how people are."

Another round of shots echoed through the hills. Luke winced. "Man, it sounds like war! You sure they're not shooting at animals?" he asked.

"No, they're not even hunters. They

couldn't hit the side of a barn if they were aiming at it. If they did hit it, it'd be an accident," Nickell said.

After waving good-bye to Nickell, Luke biked home. It was late in the afternoon, and he thought there was enough daylight left to get in an hour or so working on the new koi pond. As Luke was digging, he had the uncomfortable feeling that someone was watching him. He took a quick glance around but didn't see anyone.

My imagination, he said to himself. Just my imagination. But the uneasy feeling persisted.

Luke kept on digging, but from time to time he stopped and glanced over toward the woods. He couldn't escape the feeling that he was being watched. On a hunch, Luke turned toward the woods and called out, "Hi, Rain. Why don't you come on out of there and talk to me?"

Nothing happened. Luke called out again. "Hi, Rain. I want to talk to you about the rose garden."

Slowly the figure of a girl emerged from the woods. She had long, silky black hair and green eyes.

"Hello," she said to Luke.

"Hi, Rain," Luke said.

"How do you know my name?" she asked.

"You talked to my mother the other day. She told me all about you. She thought you were really nice. My mom's writing a book, and she is going to describe the girl in the book looking like you, because you're so pretty," Luke said.

His heart was pounding. He didn't want to make a mistake and frighten her away. He needed to find out who she really was and if she had a connection to the skeleton they had uncovered. He felt sure she did.

"Your mother is very kind," Rain said. "You said you wanted to talk about the rose garden."

"Yes. My mom said we're going to plant roses over there where the old rose garden used to be. I wonder what color roses we should get. What do you think?" Luke asked.

The girl came closer. Her big luminous eyes looked incredibly sad on closer inspection. She glanced over at the abandoned site where the first koi pond was supposed to be. "Red," she said. "Red roses are the prettiest. He liked red."

"Who did?" Luke asked eagerly.

The girl did not seem to hear the question, or else she didn't want to answer it. Finally, she spoke. "Why did they disturb the grave?" she asked. "It wasn't hurting anything. And the roses were so beautiful."

"Nobody knew there was a grave there, Rain," Luke said softly. "Uh . . . did you know the man who was buried there?"

The girl paled. She said in a trembling voice, "They'll bring him back, won't they? I mean, a person should be able to rest in peace, shouldn't he? Don't you think a person should be able to rest in peace?"

7 LUKE REPEATED the question. "Rain, did you know the man who was buried under the rose bushes?"

The girl began to look frightened. She looked like she might turn at any moment and run away. That's the last thing Luke wanted. He didn't know quite what to do to gain her confidence and get more information from her. He decided to stop asking her about the dead man and raise a more cheerful subject.

"It's very beautiful around here, isn't it, Rain?" he asked. "I've never seen a more beautiful place."

The girl nodded, but she still looked frightened.

Luke took a small step toward her and spoke very softly, "Rain, we need to know who was buried here. It's very important to know who he was. He probably had a family. They're looking for him. Could you help us find out who the man was?"

"I don't know . . . anything," the girl

said, turning. "I have to go now." With that she hurried into the woods.

Luke didn't try to follow her, but he was pretty sure that she did know the identity of the skeleton. Luke figured she was one of the people who lived at the homeless camp. Probably the victim had lived there too. Maybe there was a fight one night and the man was killed. One of those violent confrontations that sometimes happens between people.

The girl may have witnessed the murder and been traumatized by it. She was too frightened to go to the police. Or maybe even she was the one who shot the man. Maybe it was domestic abuse and she shot him in self-defense, although she still loved him.

One thing Luke was sure of—the girl knew the man who lay buried under the rose bushes, and she cared for him.

Rhea came from the house and joined Luke. "Who was that girl? I saw you talking to a girl out here," Rhea asked.

"Rain. The girl Mom talked to. I think she lives in the homeless camp," Luke said.

"Do you think she's the one we heard crying that night?" Rhea asked.

"Maybe. And she's probably the dark figure we saw darting into the woods," Luke said.

"Does she know something about the dead body?" Rhea asked.

"I think so. But she seems too scared to say anything," Luke replied.

"But she has to tell the police, Luke. Maybe you should call Sergeant Arthur and ask him to go talk to her," Rhea said.

"I've thought of that," Luke admitted, "and then I picture police cars screaming up to the homeless camp and everybody terror-struck. Who knows what might happen?"

"But, Luke, if somebody in that camp killed the guy, then that means there's a murderer running free real close to where we live! What if he comes and attacks us some night!" Rhea cried.

"You know what, Rhea?" Luke said quickly. "I'm going over to that homeless camp myself after school tomorrow. Maybe Dad can take me. I think he will."

"But that's dangerous," Rhea said. "You

should let the police do it!"

"Rhea, you saw them that day when Casey was terrorizing them. Poor ragged people. I'm going to at least give this a shot. If I tell them the *police* have to know the name of the dead guy, maybe they'll feel like they have to tell me," Luke said.

When Luke's father stepped outside, Luke told him his plan. "Okay," Luke's father said. "I'll pick you up from school. Then we'll both go down to the homeless camp and talk to Rain and any others who are living there."

"Thanks, Dad," Luke said. Luke trusted his father to handle the situation just right.

....................................................

During lunch at school the next day, Luke noticed Casey and his friends glaring at him. Before Luke came on the scene, Nickell and a friend would eat lunch with Casey and Rocky. Now everything had changed. Nickell and a friend ate lunch with Luke. Nickell said she had been getting tired of Casey Pike and his bunch even before Luke showed up, but meeting

Luke gave her just the push she needed to cut Casey off.

Casey came up to their lunch table and looked right at Nickell. "Hey, look at you packing away the macaroni and cheese. You'd better cool it with all this eating," he said. It wasn't true, of course. He was just trying to get even with Nickell for snubbing him.

"Thanks for the diet advice, Casey," Nickell said coldly. She was so slim and pretty that Casey's taunt had no effect on her.

When Luke's father picked him up after school, Luke started talking about the homeless camp. "I wonder what kind of people can live like that, Dad. Old garbage bags strung over the branches of trees for shelter. No running water. I mean, who can survive in those conditions?"

"They're misfits, Luke," Luke's father said. "I don't say that in a mean way. It's just the plain truth. They don't fit into our society. Most people can jump through the right hoops and play the game acceptably, so they fit. But some folks can't. In the old days, when your grandfather was a boy, it was easier to be a misfit."

"How so?" Luke asked as they neared the camp.

"Well, there were lots of unskilled jobs. Families were more likely to help a relative with problems. And there were cheap places to live if you didn't have a lot of money," his father replied.

"I never knew that," Luke said.

"Used to be low-cost hotels in downtown San Diego. They called them flophouses. Anybody could afford a bed. Now they've torn down all those places, and there's no place to sleep but the sidewalk," his father said.

As the car drove along, a scrawny coyote from the lower dry hills sprinted across their path.

"A coyote," Luke cried. "I've never seen one except in cartoons."

"They're misfits too," his father said sadly. "Refugees from the hills down below. Somebody is building magnificent houses down there, and they're forcing the coyote out."

"The homeless camp is around the next corner," Luke said, remembering the path

Casey took during his evil rampage.

But when they turned the corner, Luke couldn't see anybody around. There was some trash visible, but no people. Luke's father drove slowly across the meadow, then stopped.

"Well, let's each grab a garbage bag and clean this place up, Luke. It's not that bad, but to somebody coming through, a few empty milk cartons and candy wrappers are enough to fuel hatred toward these people."

In ten minutes, Luke and his father had filled two small garbage bags, and the meadow looked clean.

"I wonder where everyone is! I know this is where they usually stay," Luke said, frustrated. "They probably saw us coming from a distance and just took off," he continued.

"Probably," his father said, getting back in the truck. "How did you know this was the place? Have you been here before?"

"Well, one time Casey Pike gave Rhea and me a ride home from school, and he detoured over here. He drove his car right at a group of homeless people. Just to scare them. It was sickening," Luke said.

"Oh, I see. Well, that doesn't surprise me. Casey's father hates these homeless people," his father said.

"I wish *someone* was here! I'm pretty sure this girl, Rain, knows the identity of the dead guy, Dad. I don't know what to do," Luke said.

"We could tell Sergeant Arthur to come over here. He might be able to get some information. But I don't know if I'm comfortable with that," Luke's father said. "The chief might find out. He might tell Jim to arrest everybody in the camp and haul them off to jail for vagrancy or something. I just don't want that to happen. Maybe we should just call it a day."

"Yeah, I guess so. We tried our best," Luke answered quietly.

It was almost dark by the time they got home.

Rhea and her mother met them at the door. "What happened?" she asked.

"It was a wild-goose chase," Dad said. "The people took off before we got there."

"Sergeant Arthur came to the house while you were gone," Mrs. Payson said.

"What did he say, Ellie?" Luke's dad asked.

Mrs. Payson walked over to the coffeepot and poured two cups. "Well, it was very encouraging. You know how we thought the body had been the result of some murder? Well, Jim Arthur says they aren't so sure it was a homicide at all . . ."

"How could that be?" Mr. Payson asked, gripping his coffee cup with both hands as he did when he was in deep thought.

"Well, it might have been an accident—a hunting accident. That's what Jim said," Luke's mom said.

"Oh, and I guess the dead guy must have just buried himself then? That was real considerate of him," sneered Rhea, who was standing in the doorway.

"Don't be a wise girl, Rhea," her mom said. "Of course someone buried him. But if some hunter killed his friend by mistake, it's easy to imagine he was so distraught that he tried to get rid of the body by burying it."

Their father frowned. "I'm really surprised that Jim Arthur is taking that route. He seems like the kind of guy who digs at a case until he's got the whole story. It really disappoints me that he's reaching for the easy way out like this," their father said.

"Yeah," Luke said bitterly, "he's trying to just blow it off."

"You guys," their mother protested, "don't take that attitude! Maybe it *was* an accident. Why does it have to have been some horrible, bloody murder?"

**8** "SO NOW WHAT? Sergeant Arthur just closes the case and we bury him? I suppose they'll bury him in that part of the cemetery where they put the people who have no money," Rhea said. "Carlos told me about that. There aren't any markers or anything. 'Here lies nobody, loved by nobody, grieved by nobody.' Some poor young guy stuck in a grave with no name."

"Don't be so dramatic, darling," her mother said.

But Luke felt the same way as his sister. He was disgusted with Sergeant Arthur for not digging deeper and for trying to write it off as an accident.

Luke made up his mind that he'd make one more attempt to find Rain and get her to reveal the victim's name. She seemed to care deeply for the young man, and surely she wouldn't want him in an unmarked grave.

Luke biked down to the homeless camp

after school the next day. When he'd come with his father the day before, the roar of the engine had frightened the people away. But now, Luke came silently on his bike.

Luke rode his mountain bike to the edge of the woods overlooking the meadow where the camp was. He was heartened to see activity there. The people had come back!

But he had to be careful. If he just swooped down on them, they could scatter like they did when Casey Pike drove toward them. Luke waited patiently until he saw Rain walk to the edge of the river. He made his way slowly toward her.

"Hi, there," Luke said with a big smile.

The girl almost panicked and ran, but something in Luke's friendly face reassured her. She even cracked a little smile. "Hello," she said.

"I've come to tell you something," Luke said.

"What?" she asked. She was so pretty with her big, bright eyes and long, silky hair now highlighted by the rays of the setting sun.

"You asked me about the man who was buried in our yard," Luke said. "You wanted to know if the police would return his body so he can be buried where we found him."

The girl looked hopeful. "Will they? We can plant the roses then. I talked to your mother, and she said we could plant roses," she said.

"No, Rain, it won't be like that. Since the police don't know his name, they will take him to the town cemetery and just bury him with no marker. Nobody will know he's there," Luke said.

The girl looked horrified and distraught. "Nooo," she moaned.

"It's a part of the cemetery where they put people with no name. It's called a potter's field," Luke said. Luke hated to upset the poor girl, but he thought that it was the only way to get her to reveal the name. "The graves with nameless people."

"But he had a name," Rain said forlornly.

"If you tell me who he was, then we can get him a tombstone, Rain. His name will be on it, and we can get him a bronze vase for flowers too," Luke said. "You can put red roses in the vase anytime you want."

"But I don't have any money," Rain said. "How can I pay for a tombstone and a vase when I don't have any money? He died, and I didn't know what to do because I know it costs a lot of money to bury people. A funeral and putting somebody in a cemetery costs a lot. So my friends and I found a pretty place for him. The people who lived there were gone, and we buried him. And then later on, I asked the lady if we could put in a rose garden but I didn't tell her why. She was very nice. She and I planted the roses. It was such a pretty place for him." Tears started running down the girl's face.

"How did he die, Rain?" Luke asked gently.

"He was shot. He was down near the river fishing by himself. I found him dead. I don't know why somebody shot him. He was such a beautiful person. He had never hurt a soul in his whole life. I don't know why they shot him. My friends and I, we said some prayers and buried him. We didn't know what else to do," Rain said.

Two people from the homeless camp came walking up. A man with a gray beard, who looked about 50, and a woman who seemed to be about the same age. They both looked weary.

"Who are you?" the man asked Luke.

"My name is Luke Payson. I live in the house where the body was found. We think he was from here," Luke explained.

"You trying to make trouble for us?" the man asked, more in a frightened than angry voice.

"No. We just need to know who the man was. I want him to be buried in the cemetery with a marker," Luke said.

"Roland Kibler," Rain said. "That was my brother's name. He called himself Sky. We used to live in foster homes. Lots of foster homes. We ran away from the last one, and picked new names. We just wanted to start over. I found my name on a marker by a little stone house in the woods."

Luke felt so sad for this girl. She had obviously been through a lot. She and her brother fled a foster home and had found a safe place with these drifters. They weren't hurting anyone. Why would somebody shoot the boy?

"Did anybody see what happened when Roland got shot?" Luke asked the older man and his wife.

"No," he said. "Do you know what will happen if the police come around here asking questions? We'll all get arrested just for being alive. Rain found her brother lying by the river, cold and dead. Must have been somebody from town who did it."

The woman reached in her cloth purse for a bracelet and held it toward Luke. "This isn't worth much, but it might help a little for the boy's burial," she said.

"Ma'am," Luke said, "I believe there's a fund in town for burying people with no money. I'm sure we can do that for Roland. But didn't he have any other family?"

Rain shook her head. "We were taken from our parents years ago. I don't even remember them. We had a hard time until we came here and joined these folks. They're like family to me. We hunt and fish and sometimes we do odd jobs. We make out all right," she said.

"You know," Luke said, "the police are

looking into who killed your brother, Rain. If you know anything about who it might be, the police will arrest that person. Don't you think whoever killed him ought to pay for it?"

"Will it bring the boy back?" the older man asked. "The people in town did it. I don't know who, but probably it happened when they were recklessly firing their guns. The fool who did it might not even know what he did."

Luke biked back to town and went directly to the police station. Sergeant Arthur was at his desk.

"Hi," Luke said, "I've got some information for you. I can tell you the name of that guy we found in our yard."

"Can you really?" Sergeant Arthur asked, leaning forward in his chair.

"His name was Roland Kibler. He lived in that homeless camp out there. Rain, the boy's sister, said she found him dead by the river, shot. It looks like he might have been killed by guys who were shooting off their guns for fun. You know, like they do sometimes," Luke said.

Chief Elroy Anderson appeared in the doorway to listen to the conversation.

"The girl said they had no money so they just buried him in the Asbury yard and then planted rose bushes there," Luke said. "They did it while the Asburys were off on vacation, and nobody knew about it until my family dug there," Luke said.

"So, we got a name for our skeleton now, eh?" Chief Anderson said. He was a stout, red-faced man. "What a wacky story, eh? A skeleton in a rose garden, man alive!"

Luke resented the fact that Chief Anderson had a humorous look on his face, as if the whole thing was a joke.

"You know, some of the young guys around here go shooting all over the hills, sometimes pretty near the homeless camp," Luke said. "I bet one of them murdered the poor kid."

"Whoa, now," Chief Anderson said. "That's pretty strong language, son. We aren't calling this a homicide. It looks like an accident. A simple hunting accident. The boy was killed by a hunting rifle shot. Some fool shot him by mistake, and then got scared and took off. Easy to understand."

"Yeah, but isn't it illegal to shoot guns and kill people, even if it's an accident? Isn't that second-degree murder? Or manslaughter? Or something?" Luke demanded.

"Say," Chief Anderson chuckled, "we got a mighty savvy city boy here. You been watching a lot of crime shows on TV? What happened, most likely, is the low-life drifters were shooting squirrels, and one of them mistakenly shot the boy instead. Those people are all thieves and liars. If one of them told me the sun was shining, I wouldn't believe it unless I looked to see for myself. Since they killed one of their own, I don't think we should waste a lot of time chasing our tails over this."

Luke decided he did not like Chief Anderson at all. He remembered Nickell mentioning that Chief Anderson and Casey Pike's dad were close friends. Perhaps, Luke thought darkly, the chief suspected that Casey or his friends were responsible for the accidental shooting. And, to avoid making trouble for the Pike family, he had decided not to investigate the death.

"So, you just write 'case closed' on this guy's death without even an investigation?" Luke asked bitterly. "I mean, just because it was a guy from a homeless camp, he doesn't count, right?"

"Well," Chief Anderson said in a hostile voice, "I'll tell you what we could do. We could arrest that whole pack of homeless people out there and charge them with murder and obstruction of justice and burying a body on private land. I've a good mind to do just that. Folks around here are sick and tired of them, anyway."

It was a threat. A blunt, ugly threat.

Luke left the police station, totally disgusted. He stopped at the Community Church and talked to Reverend Plunkett, the pastor. Reverend Plunkett was in charge of community charities in Hardy. He assured Luke they would bury the young man in the town cemetery and provide a modest tombstone and a bronze vase. Reverend Plunkett said they'd take up a collection in the community.

"We need the date of birth and death, Luke," Reverend Plunkett said, "and any little message the sister would like, such as 'beloved brother.' "

Luke returned to the homeless camp the next day to gather information. Rain told him her brother had been born on October 30. He had died on November 5 of the previous year. Roland Kibler was just 17 when he had died. Just a year older than Luke was now. It sent a shaft of pain through Luke to realize that. The kid had his whole life in front of him. It was so unfair. A poor kid rejected by most of the world and then murdered, and nobody cared.

"What would you like on the stone?" Luke asked Rain.

" 'Beloved brother, rest in peace,' " Rain said. "Or is that too many words? I don't think anybody loved him but me. But I'd be thankful if you could say that."

9 "HEY, NICKELL," Luke said at school the next day. "I found out some more stuff about the guy who was buried in my yard."

"Like what?" Nickell asked.

Luke filled Nickell in on the identity of the skeleton. "Well, he was just a kid. A kid named Roland. But he called himself Sky. Seventeen years old. He hardly had a chance to live," Luke said softly.

Ms. Fischer overheard the conversation and came over. "Did you say they identified that boy you found in your yard, Luke?" she asked.

"Yeah. Roland Kibler. He lived in that homeless camp with his sister. He was only 17," Luke said.

"That's so sad," Ms. Fischer said. Nickell nodded in agreement.

"Turns out his sister, Rain, found him shot dead. She and her friends buried him in the Asbury yard when the Asburys were gone on vacation. Rain didn't have any money for a regular burial, so they just found a nice place. Reverend Plunkett said he's going to give Roland a regular burial. And a tombstone and stuff."

"Oh, that's nice," Ms. Fischer said. "I'm sure some of the students would want to help with that, since Roland is the same age as many of them. Maybe the students would be interested in donating money or something."

"That'd be great, Ms. Fischer," Luke said, gaining even more respect for the teacher.

"So do the police have any leads on who shot Roland?" Nickell asked.

"Seems like Chief Anderson has decided it was just an accident. He wants to close the case," Luke said bitterly. "I think, because Roland was homeless, Chief Anderson doesn't think his death is too important."

"But whoever killed Roland needs to be held responsible for it," Nickell cried. "Even if it was an accident. I mean, people have no right shooting off in all directions and killing people! That's reckless!"

"Luke, perhaps you could say a few

words at the assembly tomorrow," Ms. Fischer said. "That might inspire the students to donate."

"Sure, Ms. Fischer," Luke promised.

...............................................................

That day, as Luke and Rhea waited for the school bus to take them home, Casey Pike came walking along.

"So I hear they identified the skeleton," he said. Casey had a nasty smirk on his face.

"Yeah, he's been identified," Luke said.

"So what's with the burial and investigation?" Casey asked. "He was just a guy from the homeless camp. He was a nobody. They're all nobodies."

Nickell, who was waiting for the bus too, gave Casey a withering look. "What an ugly thing to say! No human being is a nobody. That boy was as important as you or me."

Casey looked embarrassed. "Well, you know what I meant. Those people sit around the river like piles of trash. They wear rags. They sleep in cardboard boxes. I mean, is that a life? The guy who got killed was lucky. He doesn't have to look in garbage pails for dinner anymore. He doesn't have to sleep in a box," he said.

"He was a human being with a right to live!" Nickell cried shrilly.

As Nickell argued with Casey, Luke noticed Rocky standing silently on the sidelines. Rocky had been listening in on the entire conversation but had said nothing. The guilt and sadness on Rocky's face caused Luke's mind to race.

Did Rocky know something about Roland's death?

Had Roland been killed by a stray shot from Rocky's gun?

Or perhaps did Rocky witness the murder?

Luke stiffened at all of the possibilities.

.......................................................................

At the assembly the next day, Ms. Fischer addressed the student body. "As most of you know, a young man's body was found in Luke Payson's yard several days ago. Well, that body has been identified as Roland Kibler, a boy who lived at the homeless camp. His family and friends buried him in a yard because they had no funds for a funeral or casket. Some members of the community have decided to give Roland a proper burial— complete with a tombstone and vase for flowers. If anybody wants to contribute money to help pay for the burial, we will have a basket up here after the assembly."

Ms. Fischer stepped away from the microphone, and Luke took her place. "You guys, I met Roland's only known relative. She's a nice girl named Rain. I got the dates of her brother's birth and death, and we're putting them on the tombstone, along with a saying she picked out. I want you guys to know that she'd be grateful for any contributions. Reverend Plunkett, from the Community Church, is going to have a little graveside service and we can all go. I think it would mean a lot to Rain if we were there."

After the assembly, as the students were dismissed, Casey sauntered up to Luke. "Boy, you're making a big deal out of this, aren't you? That skeleton has made you a celebrity. Finding those bones is the best thing that ever happened to you," he said.

Luke ignored Casey. Truth was, Luke wished the skeleton had never been found in his backyard. He would never again be able to look out his bedroom window without thinking of it and feeling sad. It cast a pall over his life.

That night, Luke stayed up late working on a science project. As he worked, he heard noises in the backyard. He expected to see an opossum, but instead he saw Rain. She was standing there in the wind, her hair blowing around her face.

Luke sprinted downstairs and ran out the back door. "Hey, Rain! Rain, what's the matter?" he called out.

"Oh, Luke," she said sadly. "They came to our camp just now and tore everything to pieces. They even stole some of our things. They said we'd better get out of there and never come back," Rain sobbed. "Two have left already—Rusty and Sarah—the man and wife you met. They're gone already. I'm going to meet them."

"Who tore your camp to pieces?" Luke demanded. "Who were they?"

"Some men in masks. They said they don't want to see us around anymore.

We're going downriver to the Bluebird Caves. We can stay there for a while," Rain said. "Please come tell me when they bury Roland, okay? I don't want to miss that."

"I'm so sorry, Rain," Luke said, anger welling up inside him. "I'll keep in touch. Are you sure you're okay now? I can get you something to eat, if you want."

"I'm okay. I have to go. Rusty and Sarah are waiting for me." And with that, she turned and ran into the woods.

Luke stood there, shaking with fury. How could someone drive human beings out of their homes? Then, suddenly, it dawned on Luke. Perhaps Roland's killer, or killers, were responsible for forcing Rain and her friends to move. Perhaps the masked men worried that Rain, or her friends, would lead police to Roland's killer.

........................................................

As Luke turned in his science project the next day, Casey tapped him on the shoulder. "What's new?"

"Nothing," Luke snapped.

"I heard some good news. Somebody

said that dirty, smelly, homeless camp cleared out last night. They must have gone somewhere else," Casey said.

"Where did you hear that?" Luke asked. He hadn't learned about the raid until near midnight when Rain came to tell him. How could Casey have known unless he was part of the raid?

"Heard it through the grapevine," Casey said.

"You're a liar," Luke whispered bitterly. "You were one of the masked men who attacked those poor people last night. You went out there and threatened them. You're afraid they will tell the police something about Roland's death!"

All during the rest of science class, Luke and Casey exchanged bitter looks. Some of the other students noticed it and expected a fight to break out between the two boys. Somebody tipped off the teacher.

"We don't want any violence around here," Mr. Ganzer warned. "We have zero tolerance for it. Anybody caught making threats or fighting gets expelled from school."

Luke did not know who to turn to. It

was an outrage that people could go to the homeless camp and drive people off. It was criminal that a boy had been shot and nobody was going to be held accountable.

Luke thought of the one person at school he could turn to, Ms. Fischer. She had a missing boy of her own. Surely she would understand the tragedy of this situation.

After science class, Luke went into Ms. Fischer's empty classroom. "Some masked cowards went to the homeless camp last night and drove those poor people out, Ms. Fischer. I'm so angry and frustrated. They can't be allowed to get away with stuff like that. It was bad enough that Chief Anderson ended the investigation, and now this! There's no justice left in this town."

"Oh, Luke, I'm so sorry," Ms. Fischer said. "You know, you're a very special young man. You have a strong sense of fairness and a lot of compassion, and that is commendable. I'm so proud of you. You'll be pleased to know we collected a nice sum to help with the young man's burial. That's largely because you took a hand in it. You can be proud of that."

"Thanks, Ms. Fischer, but what are we going to do about these masked men?" Luke asked.

"Luke," Ms. Fischer said, "please don't take what I'm about to say in the wrong way. You have such a good heart, and that's a beautiful thing. But the truth is, that homeless camp has been quite a problem in Hardy. The people are careless with their trash, and it's a health hazard. Some of the people here are afraid of those strangers. You know, they might be criminals. They might endanger our children."

Luke stared at the teacher, shocked by the direction this conversation had taken. "Has anybody from the camp ever committed any crimes in town?" he asked.

"Not yet," Ms. Fischer said carefully. "But most people in town resent them. They really do. There has even been a community meeting to discuss ways of getting them to move. That's why the generosity from the students to help pay for the boy's burial was so heartwarming.

Of course what happened last night was wrong, but if you make too much of it, then people are going to turn against you. That would be such a shame because you're really a fine young man. You're just such a great kid. I don't think this is a hill you want to climb."

It was just a figure of speech.

"The hill you want to climb."

Coming from Ms. Fischer, the words sent a chill through the marrow of Luke's bones. It reminded him of a quote he had read once. He couldn't remember the exact words, but the gist of it was—all evil needs to succeed is for good people to do nothing about it.

Evil was succeeding in Hardy very well the way Luke saw it. A young man had been shot in the head, then left by the river for wild animals to maul. And nobody in Hardy cared because the young man was not one of their own.

When Luke looked at the teacher he had once respected, he was trembling with emotion. "Ms. Fischer, they can't be allowed to get away with this," he said.

"Luke, you're right at the age when

fighting for a righteous cause makes the most sense. You're at that age when everything is so simple. You can see right and wrong so clearly, but it's not clear at all. It's gray and fuzzy. These homeless people have brought a lot of their troubles on themselves. They're lazy. They won't work. And if it's true that the boy was hit by a random rifle shot by some kids just letting off steam, well, I still say people shouldn't be *living* out there in the woods. If the boy had been living in town like a regular person, he would still be alive," Ms. Fischer said.

Luke turned and walked away from the room. He caught the bus but didn't get off at his stop. Instead, he took the bus to town, and walked into the police station. Sergeant Arthur listened sympathetically to the story of the raid on the homeless camp.

"A terrible thing," he admitted. "Those guys were bullies. Do you think the homeless folks will come in and make charges?"

Before Luke could answer, Chief Anderson emerged from his office. "If they do, I'll wager we got a few outstanding warrants on them too. Likely they're druggies or vagrants. If I were them, I'd hightail it right out of the city and count my blessings," he said. "If you're friends with them, you might want to relay that tip to them."

"So, it's okay for people to terrorize the homeless?" Luke asked, looking back and forth between Chief Anderson and Sergeant Arthur.

Sergeant Arthur looked very embarrassed. He drummed his fingers nervously on his desk. "Of course not. Theoretically, attacking the homeless is criminal behavior. But in the real world . . ."

"In the real world, you shoot a 17-year-old boy to death, and you get away with it," Luke cut in. "In the real world, you have no rights if you're not part of the town folks."

Chief Anderson glared at Luke. "You've got a real anger-control problem. You need to watch that," he said.

"But some people attacked the homeless camp last night," Luke argued.

Chief Anderson chuckled. "Nobody was

hurt from what I hear. To tell the truth, it's good that some people ran them out. Look, you're making a mountain out of a molehill," he said. "Go home and take a cold shower, and forget all this stuff."

"A guy at school knew all about the raid. There's no way he could have known unless he was part of the gang tearing up the place," Luke said stubbornly.

"And who would that be?" Chief Anderson asked.

"Casey Pike," Luke said.

"Get outta here," Chief Anderson laughed. "Casey is a fine boy. He's like my own son. His daddy and I go trout fishing every chance we get. Our two boys are like brothers, and I've known Casey since birth. Listen, I've got some advice for you. Just go home and let the people of Hardy handle their own problems. We've been doing just fine without you city folks moving in and trying to change things. Get it?"

"Yeah, I get it. Murder is okay as long as the victim was a homeless person," Luke snapped.

"There was no murder. Nothing but a hunting accident," Chief Anderson said.

"I'm getting mighty tired of your mouth, Luke Payson. It's not going to be much fun living here in Hardy, for you or your folks, if you don't wise up real fast."

As Chief Anderson spoke, Sergeant Arthur was concentrating on a pile of papers on his desk. When Luke turned to walk out, Sergeant Arthur followed him. He looked ashamed. "This is just between us, okay? If you've got anything solid, take it to Peter Ayala, the sheriff in Appleton. He's a good man." With that, Sergeant Arthur scurried back inside the office and closed the door.

# 10

AT SCHOOL THE NEXT day, Luke told Nickell how Ms. Fischer had disappointed him. "I thought she was one of the good guys. Of all people, I thought she'd encourage me to do the right thing," he said.

Nickell shrugged. "I think losing her son has changed her."

"What was her son like?" Luke asked.

"A good kid who fell into the wrong crowd."

"What kids did he hang with?"

"The usual suspects," Nickell said wryly. "Casey, Rocky, Johnny. After Ms. Fischer and her husband got divorced, it seemed like Ben was really searching for something—some sort of acceptance. And it seemed like he found it in those guys. They used to go out shooting together all the time."

"So, Ben was into shooting too? When did he disappear, anyway?" Luke asked.

"Well, one afternoon, instead of going to his dad's house, he snuck out to be with his friends. Let's see, it had to be November. Early in November," Nickell said. "Yeah, it was November 5. I remember because that's my brother's birthday. Ms. Fischer never saw him after that."

November 5. Luke felt shock waves through his body.

November 5.

..................................................................

Luke and Mr. Payson drove to Appleton that evening and stopped at the house where Ben Fischer's father lived with his new wife and daughter.

"I'm quite busy," Mr. Fischer said. "What is this all about?"

"Ben, your son," Luke said.

"Oh, he went missing a long time ago," Mr. Fischer said brusquely. He did not seem too worried.

"He went missing on November 5 of last year. On that same day, a 17-year-old boy was shot to death by some guys who were recklessly shooting," Luke said.

The man looked terrified. "I'm busy now, so good night," he said, and closed the door in their faces.

Luke and Mr. Payson drove straight to the police station. Luke remembered Sergeant Arthur's advice. *If you've got anything solid, take it to Peter Ayala, the sheriff in Appleton. He's a good man.* Luke and Mr. Payson explained the situation to Sheriff Ayala. The sheriff obtained a search warrant for the half dozen rifles that were kept in the Fischer home.

Mr. Fischer seemed shocked when the deputies came, but he offered no resistance. Over the next few days, the ballistics tests proved that a bullet from one of Mr. Fischer's rifles had entered the base of Roland Kibler's skull and killed him.

Ben Fischer's father dissolved in panic. He told the whole sad story. His son, Ben, had been out shooting with other boys. They got him into it. They were just having fun. Then Ben went away from the others. He started shooting near the river. He saw the boy, but it was too late. Ben heard the young man scream and saw him crumble into the meadow grass. Ben ran to his father's house in Appleton. He begged his father to help him out, so Mr. Fischer sent the boy 2,000 miles away to a cousin in Wyoming.

Ms. Fischer, the mother, believed her son was really a missing person until about a week ago, Mr. Fischer said. Then, when he read in the papers that the body found in Hardy had been identified and there was a police inquiry, Mr. Fischer called his ex-wife and told her that Ben had accidentally killed the boy.

Ms. Fischer agreed with her ex-husband that the best course of action was to keep quiet until it all blew over.

Ben Fischer was taken into custody at the end of the week at his cousin's home. They said he broke down and cried but was glad it was finally over. He said he hadn't had a truly happy day since it had all happened.

Ben said he was sorry.

......................................................

Luke finished the excavation for the new koi pond before the burial of Roland

Kibler. The whole Payson family dressed up and attended the service at the cemetery. There were quite a few kids from school there. After the pastor said a few words, Rain came forward and placed red roses in the bronze urn near the marker. She stepped back, tears in her eyes, and whispered something to her brother.

"Rain," Luke said softly, "it was an accident. The guy who did it feels awful."

She nodded. "I don't hate him," she said. She stood on her tiptoes and kissed Luke's cheek before she walked away with her friends from the homeless camp. They all put their arms around her comfortingly, and she seemed to be among family.

Luke Payson never saw Rain again, but he never forgot her. And he made sure the bronze urn at her brother's grave always had flowers in it.